08/04/07

W9-CJT-521

For Miguel
—BJH

tiger tales
an imprint of ME Media, LLC
202 Old Ridgefield Road, Wilton, CT 06897
Published in the United States 2006
Originally published in Great Britain 2005
By Hutchinson
An imprint of Random House Children's Books

CIP data is available
ISBN 1-58925-056-7
Printed in Singapore

1 3 5 7 9 10 8 6 4 2

I Like
Black and White

by Barbara Jean Hicks

Illustrated by Lila Prap

tiger tales

stinky

slinky

large

and small

wiggly

woolly

short and tall

stripes

patches

squares

and spots

lots and lots

and lots of
spots!

twinkly skies

snowy lands

music

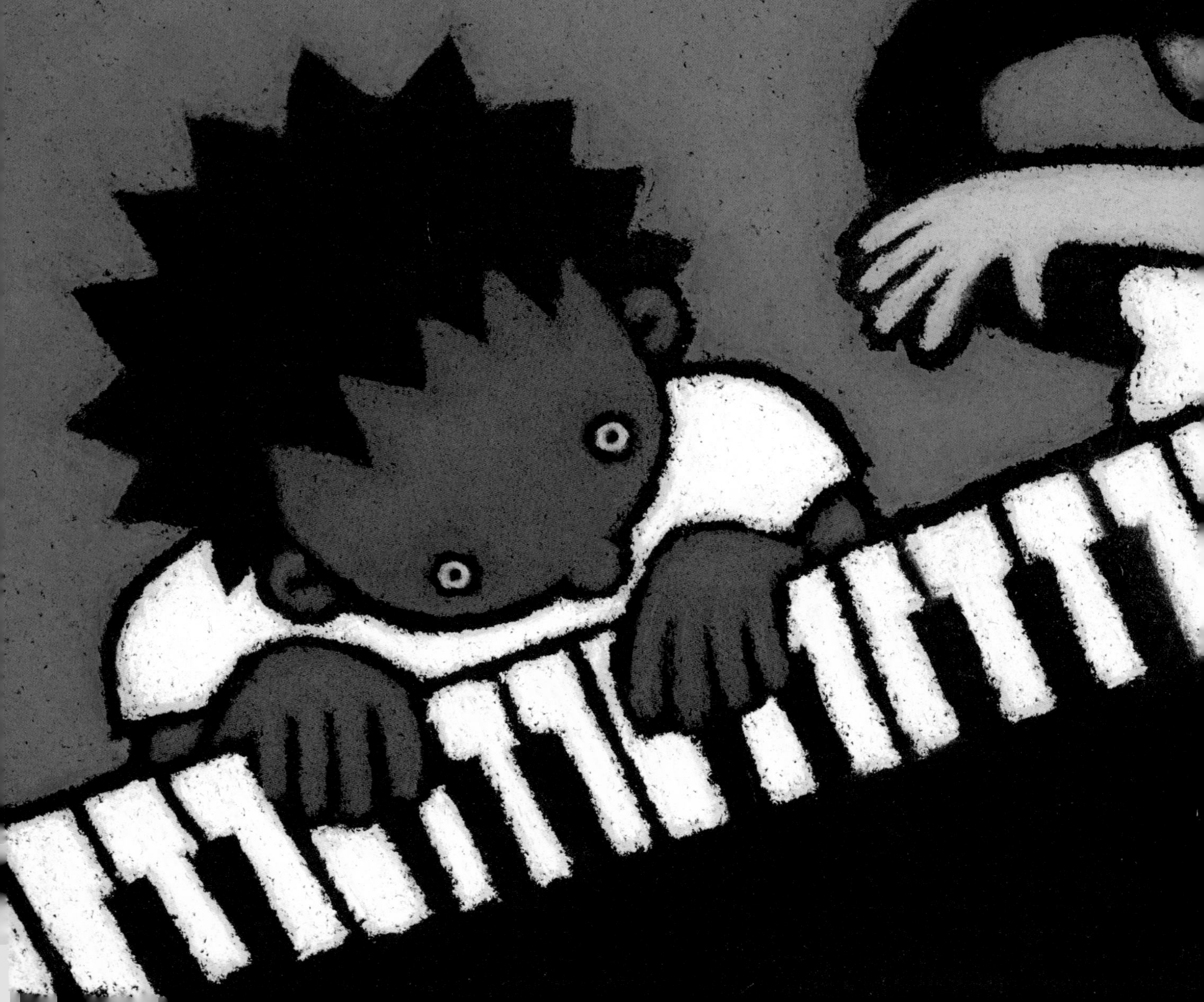

dancing

feet...